THE MISCHIEVOUS PETS

Chase Michael Kidulas

NEWMAN SPRINGS PUBLISHING
320 Broad Street
Red Bank, NJ 07701

First originally published by Newman Springs Publishing 2022

ISBN 978-1-68498-310-0 (Paperback)
ISBN 978-1-68498-311-7 (Digital)

Printed in the United States of America

To my dad. To the greatest dad a kid could ask for, Victor David Kidulas Jr. I am so grateful for him because he is a loyal, dedicated father that I know loves me very much!

1

CHAPTER 1

HOW MARY GOT HER PETS

One day, Mary was driving, and she saw a cat stuck in a tree. This little cat was meowing and clearly in distress. She decided to pull over to help the little kitty. Mary bravely climbed up the tree and rescued the cat.

On the way back home with the cat, she happened to notice a medium-sized dog stuck in the middle of the road. Mary thought to her herself, *This must be a day for rescuing!* She stopped the car and bravely crossed the street after looking to make sure no cars were coming and brought the terrified dog to safety.

All Mary could do was smile. She had never had a pet before and now she has two rescued animals she instantly fell in love with.

Along the drive home, Mary noticed something wonderful. The cat and the dog liked each other too! They sat together and if animals could talk, they would be screaming, "Thank you. We are so blessed."

The three of them played music on the way home. It was as if they had known each other forever.

CHAPTER 2

GETTING USED TO THEIR NEW HOME TOGETHER

As soon as Mary pulled into the driveway, the cat and the dog raced each other to the front door. They had never been in a house before, let alone one they could call home. But Mary noticed that the dog and cat were looking tired, and they started to cry. She quickly went to the kitchen and made them something to eat. When they were finished, they jumped on her lap and kissed her face all over.

Mary thought, *how wonderful this is*, but what should she name them? She decided on Tobey for the dog and Noah for the cat.

As they sat together, Mary noticed that they didn't smell very nice. It was time for a bath!

And that's when it all started... These little pets weren't going to be so easy to care for! They splashed in the tub, jumped out all wet, and proceeded to get water and soap bubbles all over the house!

Mary thought, "Oh boy, what did I get myself into?" The fun was on hold, it was time to train these pets!

CHAPTER 3

PROBLEM PETS!

Tobey and Noah were finally caught and dried off by Mary after practically soaking the whole house. It was time to take them out for a walk. Well, Tobey ran through the door so fast that Mary fell down. This was not okay at all. While Mary was picking herself up, she noticed Noah running off after a squirrel right out into the road! It was clear to Mary that these pets needed to be trained.

As the sun went down, the tummies started to growl. It was time for dinner.

Tobey was so fresh. He wouldn't wait for his food, he started to eat it before Mary could put it in his bowl, and Noah was even worse... Noah picked up his bowl and knocked all the food on the ground making a huge mess.

Mary was so tired from taking care of her pets. It was now time for bed and yep, you guessed it...Noah and Tobey wouldn't quiet down and fall asleep. They kept pawing at each other and biting their toys and just not settling down.

Mary thought, *I need to start training tomorrow, or I will never be able to keep them here with me!*

CHAPTER 4

TRAINING DAY

Mary woke up early the next day. She decided to watch a video on YouTube on "How to train your dog and cat." She learned that in order to get her pets to listen to her, she would need to use some *treats*! So the three of them got into the car and drove to the grocery store.

Once again, they become mischievous and knocked over the dog and cat food at the store. Mary had to clean it all up! She was so mad at them but realized that they just didn't know any better. She bought both dog and cat treats and went home to begin training.

She took them out back with a treat in hand. Mary said, "*Sit*, Tobey!" Tobey just looked at her. She then showed Tobey the treat. He was all sorts of excited, jumping everywhere trying to get it. Mary said, "*No*, Tobey! *Sit!*" She pushed his butt to the ground and then said, "Good boy," and gave him the treat. Tobey was a smart boy and learned that if he listened, he would get a treat.

Noah was a little different. Mary had to think outside of the box for this cat! It wasn't so much a treat that he paid attention to, Noah liked to play! Mary saw that Noah was watching the TV and kept jumping on the light shadows that were reflecting on the wall. Mary had a great idea! She grabbed a laser light wand! Noah followed that light everywhere and when he did, Mary then gave Noah a treat.

Mary had such a great day and a great time celebrating how well behaved her Pets had become just by spending time together training!

15

CHAPTER 5

SHARING NOAH AND TOBEY TO BRING OUT SMILES

Now that Mary's pets were trained and super well behaved, she decided to take them to work with her. Mary was a nurse at a pediatric hospital. She took care of so many children that were sick and recovering from illnesses and surgeries. Knowing that Tobey and Noah were well behaved and friendly and lovable, Mary began to introduce her pets to the children.

It was such an amazing experience to see all the children laughing, smiling, and playing with the animals. One child's experience stood out above the rest. His name was CJ, and he had recently broken his leg riding his dirt bike. It had been over three months since CJ got out of his wheelchair to walk. He was very depressed in the hospital...until...Tobey and Noah showed up!

That very same moment CJ met the pets, he stood up and walked again.

Mary was so proud of her pets, Tobey and Noah, because they were literally making miracles happen! They all went home that night with rewarding smiles because of all the good work they did.

The End

ABOUT THE AUTHOR

Chase Michael Kidulas is eight years old and in the third grade. This year, his classmates and he began reading more and more books and they really do enjoy it. He is very grateful for his father, so he decided he wanted to write him a book for a Christmas gift. He knew all he needed was his mom to help him put his story together. They talked about all the things that he loves so much including animals and helping others. This is his first book, and it really gave him an opportunity to feel like he was doing lots of good, not just for his dad but for many others too. He wants to always spread the message that one act of kindness can lead to many happy and rewarding and heartfelt scenarios. He hopes that you will enjoy reading his book as much as he enjoyed writing it with his mom.